The Wuzzles™
and the
Creepasaurs

A Story in Rhyme

by Don E. Plumme
illustrated by Bob Stuhmer

Random House 🏠 New York

Library of Congress Cataloging-in-Publication Data: Plumme, Don E. The Wuzzles and the Creepasaurs. SUMMARY: The nasty Creepasaurs plan to raid the garden of the Wuzzles and steal their Wishing Flower. [1. Gardens—Fiction. 2. Stories in rhyme] I. Title.   PZ8.3.P558694Wu   1986   [E]   85-18289
ISBN: 0-394-87877-9
Manufactured in the United States of America   1 2 3 4 5 6 7 8 9 0

The Land of Wuz is special.
It's an island in the sun,
where cuddly Wuzzles live and play
and have all sorts of fun.

The Wuzzles have a garden
full of flowers, large and small.
Butterbear knows each of them
and speaks to one and all.

Oh, the wonder of that garden
will amaze and startle you!
There's a magic Wishing Flower
that makes every wish come true.

Ah, life would be just perfect
in the distant Land of Wuz—
if only Wuzzles lived there.
Can you guess who else does?

Meet the creepy crawly Creepasaurs
and their leader, cruel King Crock.
Their heads do not think one kind thought,
and their hearts are hard as rock.

The king's sidekick, called Flizzard,
sometimes gives him good advice.
And rest assured that *his* ideas
are very rarely nice.

And now foul Flizzard had a plan
to add to King Crock's power:
"Let's wreck the Wuzzles' garden
and steal their Wishing Flower."

"A dandy scheme!" croaked old King Crock.
The Creepasaurs were excited.
"Here's how we'll do it," Flizzard said.
"I think you'll be delighted!

"The Wuzzles are all busy
playing paddlebumperball,
so let's creep right through their garden,
as if we owned it all!

"We can find the Wishing Flower
and then when we come back—
uninvited, unexpected,
we can make a sneak attack!"

As nasty Flizzard chattered
the Creepasaurs all drooled.
They thought nobody saw or heard.
But all of them were fooled.

Every bush was listening.
Every flower knew.
They heard that bigmouth Flizzard boast
of all he planned to do:

"When we return this very night
with axes, spikes, and saws,
we'll chop down everything that grows
or crush it with our claws.

"We'll steal the Wishing Flower.
Let those fuzzy Wuzzles cry.
They'll never get another wish,
no matter how they try!"

That afternoon the Wuzzles
went home without a care.
"I'll check up on my flowers,"
said gentle Butterbear.

Imagine her amazement!
Imagine her chagrin!
When she stepped into the garden,
she heard a terrible din!

The tiger lily snarled and growled!
The bluebells rang and clattered!
The feathered flower clacked and clucked!
The devil's paintbrush spattered!

"Please tell me, Wishing Flower—
I really must find out.
What's troubling the trees and plants?
What is the fuss about?

"Please try to talk. Please tell me.
I know you must know how!
Please try to talk. Please tell me.
I need your help right now!"

And then the Wishing Flower—
how very strange but true—
told all about the Creepasaurs
and what they planned to do.

In minutes all the Wuzzles
were on Creepasaur alert.
Could they save the Wishing Flower
and protect the plants from hurt?

They scratched their ears. They pulled their tails.
They wondered what to do.
"There's an answer in my pocket,
or I'm not Eleroo!"

That night the worried Wuzzles
hid near the garden gate.
King Crock and the Creepasaurs
arrived at half past eight.

"I hope this works," said Moosel.
"The Creepasaurs are strong.
I'm afraid this net we made
won't hold them very long!"

The Wuzzles aimed and tossed their trap.
The net flew through the air.
It landed on the Creepasaurs
and gave them quite a scare.

How flustered Flizzard screamed in rage
as he struggled to get free!
"A monster spider wove a web,
or so it seems to me!"

Then old King Crock took full command:
"All Creepasaurs take flight!
Get out of here as best you can
or risk that spider's bite!"

They tore the tangled net and fled,
thinking that the winner
would be whichever Creepasaur
was *not* the spider's dinner!

Now the Wuzzles chuckle softly
when they recall that night.
Their net worked in a funny way,
but did the job all right!

And in the Wuzzles' garden,
perfume still fills the air.
The plants and trees are happy,
and so is Butterbear.

The Wishing Flower listens,
as it has always done.
It still makes every wish come true
and pleases everyone.